This Walker book belongs to:

_____   _____

_____

_____

Jonah

HANDSOME HARRY ★

WINKIE THE ONE-EYED BEAR

Pumpie

THE MAHARANA OF MEWAR

Falooda

WOOLWORTH THE WOOLLEN OWL

Wee Scottie the Wind-up Dog

Augusta Marianna

Pip

MR JOLLYBOY

To Edward, William and Tilly.

With thanks to Lisa Yates for her idea of setting a story
in the Museum of Childhood.

*There is a magical toy museum in Bethnal Green in the East End of London,
called the Museum of Childhood which I visited often when I was young.
It is full of hundreds of toys, old and new, and although there was only room
in this book for some of my favourites – you will find all of them
somewhere in the Museum if you visit one day.*

First published 2011 by Walker Books Ltd, 87 Vauxhall Walk, London SE11 5HJ

This edition published 2011

2 4 6 8 10 9 7 5 3 1   © 2011 David Lucas

The right of David Lucas to be identified as author/illustrator of this work has been asserted by him
in accordance with the Copyright, Designs and Patents Act 1988

This book has been typeset in Berkeley Old Style   Printed in China

British Library Cataloguing in Publication Data: a catalogue record for this book is available from the British Library

ISBN 978-1-4063-3206-3   www.walker.co.uk

DAVID LUCAS

LOST
in the
TOY
MUSEUM

—an adventure—

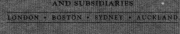
WALKER BOOKS
AND SUBSIDIARIES
LONDON · BOSTON · SYDNEY · AUCKLAND

When the lights went out at the Toy Museum
and the doors were locked,
all the toys *woke up*.
They bounced down off the shelves,
giddy and laughing
and squeaking with delight.

Jonah

Falooda

the cot

R
BOY

But Bunting, the old toy cat,
just rolled his eyes and sighed.
He brushed his whiskers,
he stretched,
and slowly, slowly,
he got down from the shelf...

TH THE
OWL

"Please assemble for inspection,"
said Bunting, just as he did every night.

He called the register,
and then he counted all the toys ...
twice ... just to be sure no one was missing.

He made sure that they
did their exercises.

He made sure that none of them
were broken or coming apart
at the seams.

And then he began to talk
about the history of the Museum
– just as he did every night.

But *that* night was different.
That night all the toys just ran away.

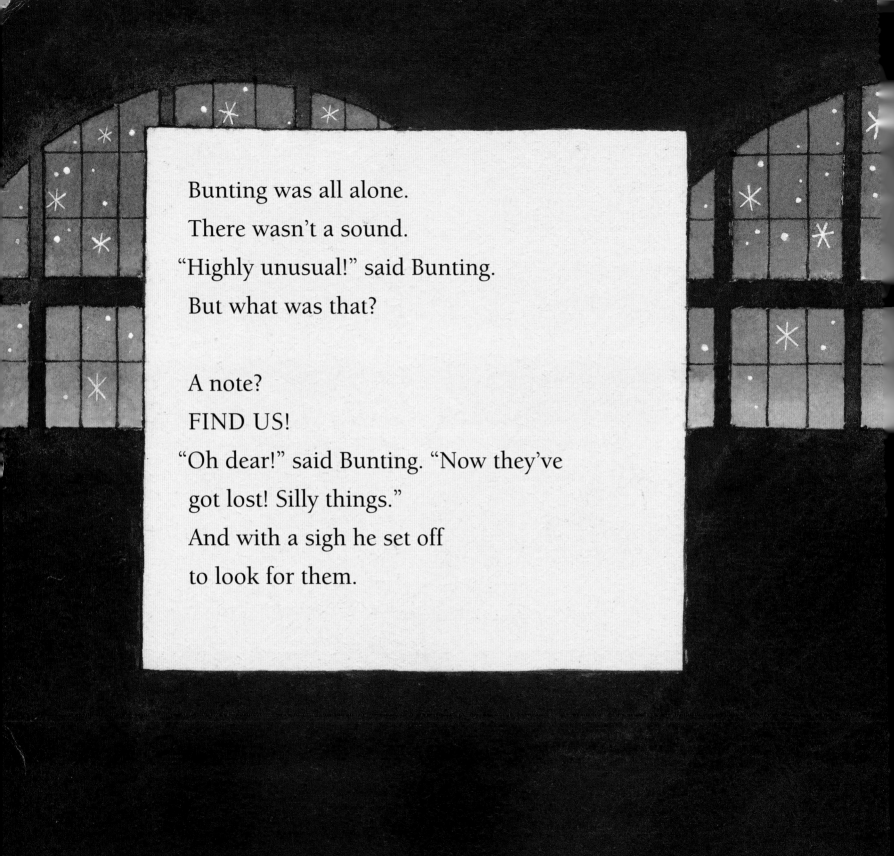

Bunting was all alone.

There wasn't a sound.

"Highly unusual!" said Bunting.

But what was that?

A note?

FIND US!

"Oh dear!" said Bunting. "Now they've
got lost! Silly things."

And with a sigh he set off
to look for them.

He looked for them everywhere.
They weren't in any of
the Dolls' Houses.

They weren't
in the Chinese Rock
Garden.

They weren't riding
on the Toy Railway.
Perhaps they were in the
Toy Theatre?
Bunting investigated.
There was a mysterious note:
GETTING WARMER.
But what did it *mean*?

He walked back through the scenery,
further than he'd ever dared go before.

And there was another note:
AND WARMER...
But what did it mean?

Then he heard
voices on the wind,
coming from across the sea.

He set sail.
He was alone on the water,
under the stars.
Now *he* was lost.
He didn't know *where*
he was at all.

But there was a message
in a bottle.
One word: COLDER.

Bunting turned
the boat around.
There, *at last*, was land!

And another note:
HOT! HOT! HOT!
(nearly on fire!!!).

"SURPRISE!"

all the toys leapt out of nowhere.

"Do you mean it's been a *game*, all along?"
  said Bunting.
"It *was* fun," they said, "wasn't it?"
"*Fun?*"
  Hmmm. Yes, he had to admit it *had* been fun.
  He'd been on an *adventure*.

"It's called *hide and seek*,"
  said the toys.

"Perhaps we could play it
  tomorrow night too?"
  said Bunting.

And now it was getting light.

But before they all hurried
back to the shelves
where they belonged,
Bunting called the register,
and counted them, *twice* ...
just to be sure.

Jonah

HANDSOME
HARRY

WINKIE
THE
ONE-EYED
BEAR

Pumpie

THE
MAHARANA
OF
MEWAR

Falooda

WOOLWORTH THE
WOOLLEN OWL

Wee Scottie
the Wind-up Dog

Augusta
Marianna

Pip

MR
JOLLYBOY

Other titles by David Lucas

ISBN 978-1-4063-2459-4

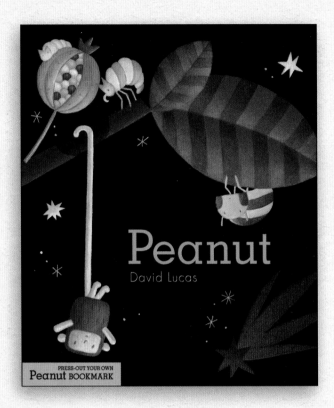

ISBN 978-1-4063-1958-3

Available from all good booksellers

www.walker.co.uk